GIRLZROCK

Dog on the Loose

Holly Smith Dinbergs

illustrated by
Chantal Stewart

First published in 2006 by
MACMILLAN EDUCATION AUSTRALIA PTY LTD
627 Chapel Street, South Yarra, Australia 3141

This edition first published in the United States of America
in 2006 by MONDO Publishing.

For information contact:
MONDO Publishing
980 Avenue of the Americas
New York, NY 10018

Visit our web site at http://www.mondopub.com

06 07 08 09 10   9 8 7 6 5 4 3 2 1

ISBN 1-59336-939-5 (PB)

Series created by Felice Arena and Phil Kettle
Project Management by Limelight Press Pty Ltd
Cover and text design by Lore Foye
Illustrations by Chantal Stewart

Printed in Hong Kong

GIRLZROCK!
Contents

Jess   Sophie

CHAPTER 1

Out for a Walk

Sophie and Jess are fast asleep on
the floor of Jess's bedroom. Jess's
cocker spaniel puppy, Sammy,
comes up to Jess and licks her face.

Jess (yawning) "Sammy, I'm trying
  to sleep!"

With half-open eyes, Jess pats
Sammy's neck and glances at the
lump lying beside her.

Jess "You awake, Soph?"
Sophie (mumbling) "Kinda."

Sophie pushes down the top of the
sleeping bag.

Sophie "Hey, I totally forgot where I was. I thought I was camping out in a tent like we did last summer."

Jess "Only this is better. We didn't get rained on and the bathroom's just down the hall."

Sophie (laughing) "Yeah, and we get to sneak into the kitchen and raid the cookie jar."

As Sophie stretches, the puppy
walks over and sniffs her head.

Sophie (giggling) "Sammy, stop
  licking me. That tickles!"
Jess "He never gives up! Sammy,
  leave Sophie alone."

Sophie "I wish I could have more
pets but Dad says I'm only allowed
to have a cat."

Jess "But you're lucky. Puffles is so
cute."

Sophie "Yeah, but your room's like a
zoo! Except that it doesn't stink."

In her room, Jess has three goldfish,
two hermit crabs, and a parakeet.

Jess "I'm starving."

Sophie "Then let's eat."

Jess "Okay, but Sammy really wants
to go outside, so we'll have breakfast
after his walk. Wanna come?"

Sophie "Sure. Race ya!"

The girls get dressed and go to the laundry room with Sammy close behind.

Jess "Here, boy. Let me put your leash on."

As Jess stuffs a plastic bag in her pocket, Sophie sees a note on top of the washing machine.

Sophie "Hey, there's a note from your mom."

Jess "What does it say?"

Sophie "She's gone shopping, and your dad's next door."

Jess "It's okay. We'll be back before them."

Sammy yanks the girls out the door.

CHAPTER 2

That Darned Cat

Jess, Sophie, and Sammy head across the yard and into the lane. Sammy starts to sniff the ground.

Sophie "He smells something."
Jess "He's looking for the right spot."
Sophie "The right spot? Like where somebody dropped a hamburger?"

Jess "No, where he can go...y'know!"

Sophie "Oh, yeah. Cats are different. They just go in the garden or a box."

The girls wait as Sammy goes. A few seconds later, Jess takes the bag out of her pocket to clean up the poop.

Jess "Here, hold the leash for a sec."

Sophie "Isn't that gross? Cleaning up poop like that?"

Jess "Nope, not when it's your own dog. And see? I'm not actually touching anything."

Sophie "No, and I guess it's better than leaving a mess on the street for someone to step in."

While Jess is cleaning up, a huge ginger cat jumps off the fence in front of them and hisses at Sammy.

The cat races off and Sammy follows, jerking the leash out of Sophie's hand. As Sammy disappears around a corner, the girls yell out.

Jess "Sammy, come back! SAAAM-MEEEE!!"
Sophie "SAAAM-MEEEE!"

Sophie "Doesn't he come if you call?"

Jess "Sometimes, but he's only a
puppy and he's still learning."

Sophie "I guess a runaway cat
doesn't help much either."

Jess "Mom's just starting to teach
him all that stuff. C'mon, we gotta
find him!"

The girls run down the lane in search of Sammy, shouting out his name as they go.

Jess "SAAAM-MEEEE! C'mere, boy!"
Sophie "He's gotta be around here somewhere. He was here only a minute ago so he couldn't have gone very far."

CHAPTER 3

Squeak in the Park

The girls race around the corner only to find an empty street.

Jess "I don't see him down here."

Sophie "Nope, he must've kept going."

Jess "Oh, no! We'll never find him. He's gone."

Sophie "It's all my fault. What if..."

Jess "What if what?"

Sophie "What if there's a storm? He's just a puppy. He'll probably be afraid of thunder. I've heard that lots of dogs are afraid of thunder."

Jess "Sophie, see that big yellow thing in the sky? It's called the sun. I don't think it'll rain anytime soon."

Sophie "I hope not. But how will Sammy find his way home?"

Jess "That's what worries me."

Sophie "I wish we had wings. Then we could fly around and find him."

Jess "Get real. Hey, I know! Sammy always comes running to play when I squeeze his squeaky mouse. And we always go to the park together, so maybe he'll go there."

Sophie (excitedly) "Good thinking! He's probably at the park. Let's go."

Jess "But we have to go home first and get the squeaky mouse. I'm sure it'll help."

The girls go back to Jess's house and get the mouse. On the way to the park, they shout Sammy's name and squeeze the plastic toy. *Squeak!*

Jess "Sammy! C'mere boy!"
Sophie "Sammy! C'mere!"

At the park, the girls see some kids and dogs, but there's no sign of Sammy.

Sophie (disappointed) "What if he's been kidnapped?"

Jess "What do ya mean? Guys in masks stealing my dog? That's dognapping, not kidnapping."

Sophie "Don't joke about it! I feel terrible. This is all my fault."

Jess "Don't worry, Soph. We're gonna find him. We just need some help."

Sophie and Jess ask some kids playing in the park to help find Sammy. Soon, they are all walking around calling Sammy's name. Meanwhile, Jess notices a poster on the fence.

Jess "Soph, I know what we can do to find him."

CHAPTER 4

Posters, Please

The girls run back to Jess's house, squeezing the mouse and calling Sammy's name.

Jess "I'll get some paper and markers. We're gonna make posters."
Sophie "Good idea!"

Jess disappears for a minute, then
returns with the paper and markers.

Jess "What should we write?"
Sophie "How about 'Have you seen
this dog?' in really big letters."

They each write the words on their
paper.

Jess "We need to offer a reward."

Sophie "But how much can we pay?"

Jess "I dunno. How much do you have?"

Sophie "I've got fourteen dollars and thirty-five cents."

Jess "I have about eleven dollars."

Sophie "Let's just write 'Reward' and not say how much."

Jess "Cool."

Jess "What else should we write?"

Sophie "Nothing, but we need a picture of Sammy. Do you have a photo of him?"

Jess "Uh-uh. We'll have to draw him."

Each girl draws a picture of Sammy. Sophie shows hers to Jess.

Jess "That's not Sammy. That's an alien dog. Here, look at mine, it's better."

Sophie "Umm...sorry, but that looks like a dark blob with eyes."

Jess "Is this really gonna help, this poster stuff? I'm getting worried. He must be really scared by now. He's just a puppy."

Sophie "We need a real picture, not a drawing."

The girls hear a car door shut.

Jess "Mom's home. She'll be so mad at us for losing Sammy, but at least she'll know what to do."

Just then, there's a knock on the back door.

CHAPTER 5

Home Sweet Home

Jess hears a bark. The girls look outside and see Sammy.

Jess "It's Sammy! He's home!"

Sophie "And it's the kids from the park. They must've found him!"

Jess flings open the door. She picks up her puppy and gives him a huge hug, while he excitedly tries to lick her.

Sophie "Sammy, you're back! I'm so glad you guys found him."

Jess "Thanks so much, guys. You're heroes! I'm psyched that Sammy's home again."

The girls say goodbye to their friends and take Sammy inside. Jess finds her mom putting away the groceries in the kitchen.

Jess "Mom, you'll never guess what happened."

Sophie "I think she probably knows. We left the posters out, remember?"

Jess "We took Sammy out while you were at the store, and he saw this cat and got really excited, and before we knew it he'd run off and..."

Sophie "Well, we thought we'd lost him forever but these kids at the park found him and brought him home."

Jess "He's had a tough morning, Mom. So can he have a treat?"

Jess's mom pulls out a bag of doggy treats.

Jess "Hey, Soph, watch this! Sammy, sit. Now shake."

Sammy sticks his paw out, which Jess shakes. Jess gives the puppy his treat and pats his head.

Jess "How good is that!"

Sophie "What a smart puppy!"

Jess eyes the groceries as her mom unpacks them.

Jess "Mom, I'm starved. We're so ready for breakfast. What do you want to eat, Soph?"

Sophie "I really don't mind, as long as it's not dog biscuits!"

GiRLZ ROCK!
Dog Lingo

Jess

Sophie

breed A kind of dog, for example, a cocker spaniel or a collie.

dognapping When a thief steals a dog and then demands money from the pooch's owner to give the dog back.

dog show A beauty contest for dogs.

dog tag Identification for your dog. It is a small piece of plastic or metal, which you attach to your pooch's collar and that has all its important info, in case it gets lost.

pooper scooper A little shovel used to clean up dog poop.

veterinarian A doctor for animals.

GIRLZROCK!
Dog Musts

☆ Be a responsible dog owner by making sure your dog is trained, fed daily, exercised regularly, kept clean, and loved.

☆ Get a good book that tells you how to care for dogs.

☆ Make sure you get a license for your dog. This license says your dog has gotten its shots—it doesn't mean your dog can drive a car!

☆ Take poop bags with you whenever you take your dog for a walk— nobody wants to step in dog poop!

☆ Before patting a dog you don't know, ask its owner for permission.

☆ Take your dog to the veterinarian every year for a check up, and be sure to get your pooch the shots and medicines it needs.

☆ Take an obedience course with your puppy as soon as the vet says it's okay. With early training, your dog won't grow up to do crazy stuff that could upset people!

☆ Take your dog for regular walks and play with it as much as you can. Dogs who are bored or need attention often misbehave (just like people)!

GIRLZ ROCK!
Dog Instant Info

There are hundreds of different dog breeds (kinds of dogs).

Of all a dog's senses, its sense of smell is the most developed. A dog's sense of smell is around 50 to 100 times stronger than a human's.

Certain human foods are really bad for dogs. Eating chocolate, raisins, or grapes can make dogs really sick.

Chanda-Leah, a toy poodle, holds the record for the dog that can do the most tricks. She can perform 469 tricks, including playing the piano, fetching a tissue if you sneeze, and untying the knot in your shoelace.

A greyhound holds the world record for the Dog High Jump. In 2003 Cindy jumped over a bar set at a height of 66 inches (167.6 centimeters).

In 2005 a Great Dane named Gibson was named the world's tallest dog. When standing upright on his hind legs, Gibson stands 7 feet (2.1 meters) tall.

In 2004 a Neopolitan mastiff in England named Tia set the world record for the largest litter when she gave birth to 24 puppies!

GIRLZROCK!
Think Tank

1 What causes Jess's dog Sammy to run off?

2 What does Jess say always gets Sammy to come running?

3 What does Sophie think might've happened to Sammy?

4 What should you do if your dog gets sick or hurt?

5 What is a dog's most developed sense?

6 If Sammy hadn't been found, what do you think Jess and Sophie would have done next? Then what?

7 Where do you think the kids who brought back Sammy found him? Why do you think that?

8 What do you think Jess and Sophie learned from this experience?

Answers

How did you score?

- If you got most of the answers correct, you're probably already planning to go to veterinary school!

- If you got more than half of the answers correct, think about becoming a dog walker. You can make some pocket money after school and on weekends.

- If you got less than half of the answers correct, get a goldfish or a bird for a pet instead of a dog!

Hey, Girls!

I love to read and hope you do too! The first book I really loved was a book called "Mary Poppins." It was full of magic (way before Harry Potter) and I got hooked on reading. I went to the library every Saturday and left with a pile of books so heavy I could hardly carry them!

Here are some ideas about how you can make "Dog on the Loose" even more fun. At school, you and your friends can be actors and put on this story as a play. To bring the story to life, bring in some props from home such as a stuffed dog to be Sammy or a toy that squeaks when you squeeze it. Maybe you can set up a small table with markers and white paper for the poster scene.

Who will be Sophie? Who will be Jess? Who will be the narrator? (That's the person who reads the parts between Sophie or Jess saying something.) Once you've decided on these details, you're ready to act out the story in front of the class. I bet everyone will clap when you are finished. Hey, a talent scout from a television station might just be watching!

See if somebody at home will read this story out loud with you. Reading at home is important and a lot of fun as well.

You know what my dad used to tell me? Readers are leaders!

And remember, Girlz Rock!

Holly Smith Durbeys

GIRLZ ROCK!

When We Were Kids

Holly   Jacqueline

Holly talked to Jacqueline, another *Girlz Rock!* author.

Jacqueline "Have you ever owned a dog?"

Holly "When I was really little, I had a French poodle named Pierre. Later, I had two cocker spaniels, Sammy and Victoria."

Jacqueline "Did you ever enter your dogs in a dog show?"

Holly "Nope. They wouldn't sit or stay where they were supposed to."

Jacqueline "So they couldn't have won any prizes for most obedient dog?"

Holly "No, but I could have won a prize for most poop scooped!"

GIRLZROCK!
What a Laugh!

Q What do you call a dog who loves bubble baths?

A A shampoodle!